Daniel

and

His Walking Stick

Published by

PEACHTREE PUBLISHERS
1700 Chattahoochee Avenue
Atlanta, Georgia 30318-2112

www.peachtree-online.com

ISBN 1-56145-330-7

Illustrations created in transparent watercolor on Arches 140 # hot press 100% rag paper;
text typeset in Adobe Baskerville; titles typeset in Adobe Beach.

Book design by Loraine M. Joyner

Printed in Singapore
10 9 8 7 6 5 4 3 2 1
First Edition

Library of Congress Cataloging-in-Publication Data

McCormick, Wendy.
 Daniel and his walking stick / written by Wendy McCormick ; illustrated by Constance R. Bergum. — 1st ed.
  p. cm.
 Summary: Jesse does not remember either of her grandfathers, but misses them anyway until her family visits
the countryside to see where Jesse's mother grew up, and they meet a very special man with a very special stick.
 ISBN 1-56145-330-7
 [1. Grandfathers—Fiction. 2. Country life—Fiction.] I. Bergum, Constance Rummel, ill. II. Title.

PZ7.M4784144Dan 2005
 [E]—dc22

2004017657

With love for Bob,

who walked with me into the Big Woods,

and to Ray and Rosa, good friends we found there

—W.M.

To my mentor and dear friend Sister Cor Immaculata Heffernan

—C.R.B.

Daniel

and

His Walking Stick

WRITTEN BY WENDY McCORMICK

ILLUSTRATED BY CONSTANCE R. BERGUM

Ω

PEACHTREE
ATLANTA

I don't have a grandfather—
Not like everyone else I know,
Not anymore.

Sometimes, when my mom brushes my hair into a braid,
She tells me about my grandfathers.

Sometimes, when I help my dad make pancakes
    on Saturday mornings,
He tells me about my grandfathers.

I had two—
Grandpa Jack, who died before I was born,
And Grandpa Ray, who lived long enough to visit me
when I was a baby.
He gave me a bath and tickled my earlobes
And sang me songs about the sea.
I don't remember it,
But that's what Mom and Dad tell me.

My dad asked if I minded
not having grandfathers.
"No," I said.
But I did.

One day last summer, Mom said,
"Jesse, we're going to the country on vacation,
Where I used to go with *my* mom and dad when I was a little girl."

As we drove away, I watched our city get smaller and smaller
until it looked like a postcard out the window.
Then I fell asleep.

When I woke up, we were in the country—
No subway, no buses. Nothing but woods all around us.
"Can you hear the wind whistle through the trees?" Mom said.
I closed my eyes, listening.

I heard footsteps, crunching leaves.
When I opened my eyes
I saw something walk out of the woods.
At first, I thought it was a tree,
come to life.

Then I saw it was an old man,
dressed in a green jacket
and brown boots,
Carrying a big gray pole.

"This is Mr. Stockton," said Mom.
  "He lives down the road."
"He taught your mom how to fish
  when she was your age," said Dad.

"You look like a tree," I said.

Mr. Stockton bent to look me in the eye.

"Thanks." He smiled. "You can call me Daniel."

"What's your pole for?" I asked.

"It's my walking stick," said Daniel,
"for walking in the woods."
He thumped the stick on the ground.

"Where'd you get it?" I asked.

"Ah…now that's a story,"
Daniel said, "that can't be
told until just the right time."

"When's the right time?"
I asked.

"Not just now," Daniel
said. "Not just now."

So, Mom and Dad and Daniel and me walked
  all along the lakeshore.
And we talked, too, about all the shiny fish Mom
  and my grandfather and Daniel used to catch.

That night Mom said, "There's nobody like that
  Daniel Stockton."
I said, "I wonder where he got his walking stick."
And I fell asleep.

The next day, Mom taught Dad how to fish,
And Daniel and me and his walking stick
went walking.

"I use my stick to pull me up hills," Daniel said,
"and to lead me down again."
"When I want to cross a stream, I slip my stick
into the water, like this, to see how deep it is."

"Why?" I asked.
"So I know if I can cross the stream
without getting my knees wet."
He winked at me.
I liked Daniel.

After that, Daniel and me and his walking stick went walking every day.

And he pointed out things that I'd never seen before—
"There," he said, and I saw a loon's nest
    with two brown speckled eggs inside.

"Over there," he whispered, and I saw a blue heron
    standing thin as a shadow at the shore.

"Here." He poked his stick into a hole in the ground.
"Here's where a woodchuck lives."

One day, Daniel used his walking stick to push back
the thorny branches of a raspberry patch so I could
get in to pick the berries.
We sat on a big, round rock to eat them.
And I told him all about my grandfathers.

"Grandpa Jack died before I was born," I said,
"And Grandpa Ray lived long enough to visit
me when I was a baby.
He gave me a bath and tickled my earlobes
And sang me songs about the sea."

"That would be just like your grandfather," Daniel said.
"The one that I knew, anyway."

"I didn't know my grandfathers," I said.
"Do you mind that?" Daniel asked.
"Yes," I said.

Daniel tapped a raspberry branch.
Some of the berries fell right into my hands.

"Could I have three grandfathers?" I asked.
"Hmm…" Daniel scraped mud off his boot
    with his walking stick.

"Why not?" he said.
"Good," I said.

Daniel stood up slowly.

"Do you want to know where I found my walking stick?" he asked.

"Is this the right time?" I asked.

"Yes," Daniel said.

So Daniel and me followed the lakeshore to the bay
   where the biggest birch tree stood.

He knelt down where the tree roots dug into the shore.
   He put his hand on the white bark.
   "Here," he said. "Here's where I found it.
      Your grandfather and I fished here sometimes."

I looked down at his hand.
   It looked a lot like those birch tree roots
      dug into the shore.

"My walking stick probably washed up
   from across the lake," he said.
"Maybe a woodchuck left it here for
   you," I said.
"Maybe." He reached down into the
   bushes near the tree.
"It looks like a woodchuck must've
   left one for you, too."

Daniel handed me a walking stick.

After our vacation, when I got home to the city,
I used my walking stick to pull myself up the steps of the bus
And to lead me down the escalator to the subway
When I went to visit Grandma Rosa.

Sometimes I pointed out things to Mom and Dad.
"There," I said, "someone left one black shoe near the flower shop."

"There," I said, "there's an airplane,
high up in the sky."

Sometimes, I used my walking stick to find out
how deep the puddles were in the street.
"Why do you do that, Jesse?" Dad asked.
"So I know if I can cross the puddle without
getting my knees wet," I said.

And then, I told my mom and dad all about my grandfathers.
I had three—

Grandpa Jack, who died before I was born,
And Grandpa Ray, who lived long enough
    to visit me when I was a baby
And tickle my earlobes and sing me songs
    about the sea.
And one, only one, called Daniel—

Who has a walking stick just like mine.

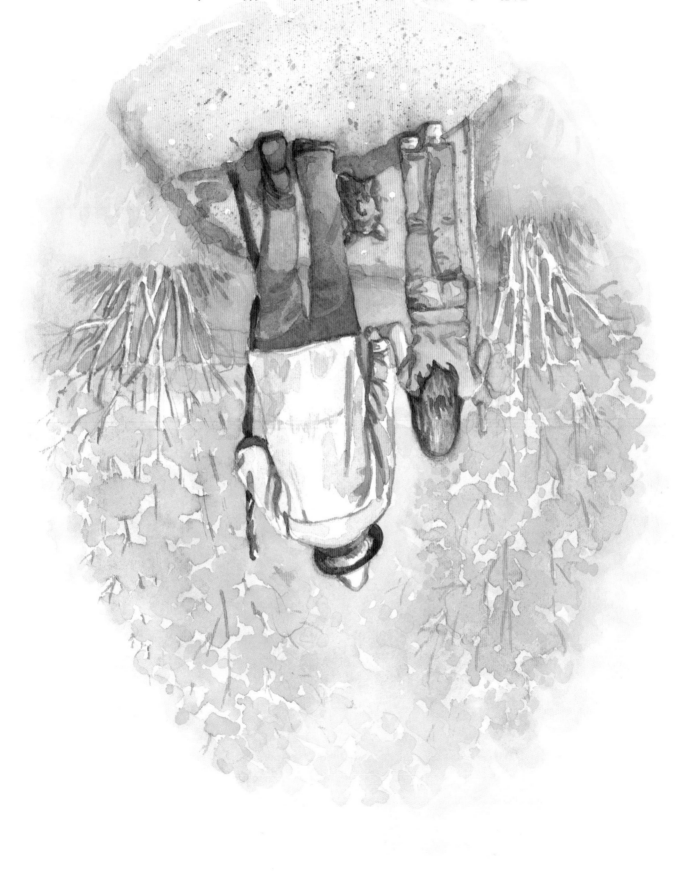